Ellie Camps under the Stars

Coauthor Elle Fair

Coauthor Marci Fair

Assistant Editor Chloe Fair

Cover & Layout Designer Nelly Murariu

I love to be outdoors
in nature—at the beach, at a park,
and even in my own backyard. I like to lie on
the grass and watch the clouds. My friends and
I can get caught up on our phones or electronics
sometimes. Outside I love to run around, play soccer,
feel the warm sunshine and enjoy nature—it's full of
interesting plants, animals, and adventures.

Have fun playing outside with
your siblings and friends!

Elle Fair, age thirteen

Ellie and Pudgy loved to play outside. Nature (what we call plants, animals, and the Earth) is interesting and full of adventures!

One day, they decided to go on a camping trip. They wanted to sleep outdoors, under the stars.

Ellie and Pudgy packed everything they would
need for the trip and then hiked until they found
the perfect place to set up their campsite.

The grass was so green, and the trees were so tall.

It was not easy to set up their tent. It twisted and turned. Ellie laughed when the wind blew it upside down.

Is that where the top of the tent should be?

Finally, they got it right. After Ellie and Pudgy unrolled their sleeping bags, they put out their camping gear and climbed into their cozy tent.

6

After they set up the tent, it was time for a hike through the woods. They heard birds chirping and bugs buzzing. They were not sure if they were strong enough for a long hike, so they started with a short one.

Some rocks were so small that they could throw them. Some were so big that they could climb them.

Do you like to climb big rocks?

Around the corner
and over a small
bridge was a secret
path. They climbed
up the log stairs
to see what they
might find.

At the top they found a road that led to an old wooden bridge. The wind whistled through the trees as they walked across the bridge to peer over the edge.

A creek ran under the bridge, rushing down the rocks on the side of the mountain.

What a great hike! Ellie and Pudgy were surprised to find they were not tired at all.

A yellow butterfly flew by to welcome them to the woods.

Can you find the butterfly in the photo?

As the sun set, Ellie and Pudgy walked back to their campsite. They talked about all the bugs, birds, and fun things they had seen. Nature was more alive and active than they had known.

12

Now it was time to eat. Hiking outside made them hungry! Ellie set the plates out on their picnic blanket while Pudgy grilled sandwiches. They were careful to clean up after dinner. They did not want animals living nearby to get hurt eating the food or to forget what they were supposed to eat.

After dinner it was game time! Ellie liked to play cards and roll the dice.

Pudgy loved to play word games. They both
spelled special words with their letters.

As it cooled off, Ellie and Pudgy built a fire to keep them warm. They wanted to make their favorite camping dessert—s'mores!

How many marshmallows does Pudgy have?

16

They put together the chocolate,

marshmallows, and

graham crackers. Ellie ate hers and

said she wanted *s'more!*

17

As the sky grew darker, they turned on their lantern and flashlight. Animal friends joined them from the woods.

What kinds of animals joined them?

When the first star twinkled against the
night sky, they said their favorite poem together
and made a wish.

"Star light, star bright,
first star I see tonight,
I wish I may,
I wish I might,
have the wish I wish tonight!"

19

ORION

The skies started to glow with more stars. Ellie told Pudgy the bright stars formed constellations, or pictures, in the night sky.

Above them,
Orion and the
Big Dipper
sparkled in the
blue darkness.

BIG
DIPPER

21

After looking at the stars for a while, Ellie and Pudgy decided to read some of their favorite books and go to sleep.

What do you like to read before you go to sleep?

22

They fell asleep while listening to the night sounds, dreaming of their new friends and camping adventures.

23

Pudgy made a healthy
breakfast to give them energy
for another fun outdoor day!
After eating, they cleaned up
their campsite.

Now they knew they were strong, so they hiked farther. They heard water coming down the mountain and then found their first waterfall.

26

The cool water tickled Ellie's face as it splashed over the edge of the rocks.

27

It was so exciting.
They kept hiking over bigger rocks
and then down onto a path
in between them.

Then they heard a roaring
and crashing sound.

Can you
spot what they
heard roaring?

29

It was a really big waterfall that
sounded like loud
waves splashing on the beach!

The waterfall's big spray cooled them off as they walked behind the falls.

What do you think the waterfall spray felt like?

31

After exploring the waterfall, they hiked up the mountain until they could see a beautiful view. The sky was so blue, and the clouds looked so big and fluffy.

The valley below was full of green trees that looked like a soft blanket covering the mountains.

33

Behind them a rock
path wove through
the woods. Ellie and
Pudgy wondered
where this path
might take them.

When they came through the woods, they were on top of a big rock mountain.

They felt like they could touch the clouds and see for miles and miles.

35

When they started their trip, Ellie and Pudgy had not been sure if they could go on a long hike or if it would be too dark camping out at night. But they had found the courage again to go and try something new.

Ellie and Pudgy learned that they were stronger than they had thought and that nature was more amazing than they had known. They would remember all of their adventures for the rest of their lives.

Help the squirrel find the way to camp.

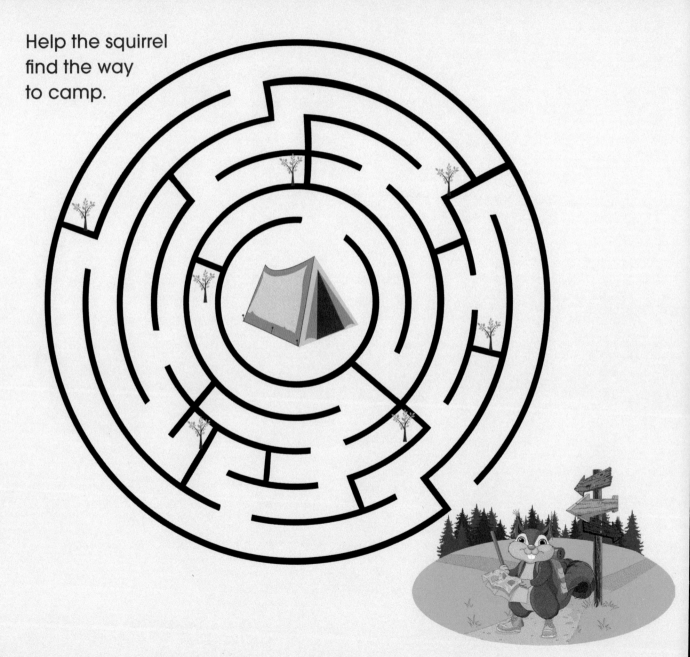

Invite a friend to play a game!

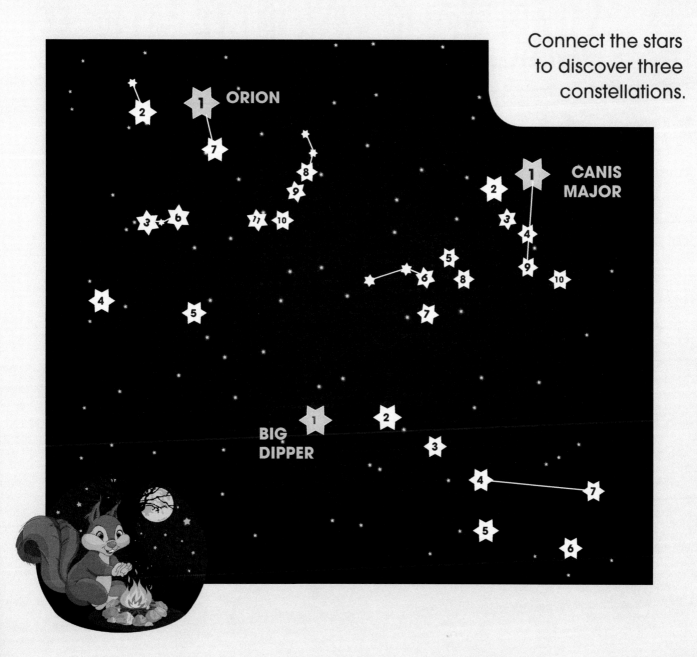

Connect the stars to discover three constellations.

SHARE YOUR FAVORITE STUFFED

1

Set up your favorite
stuffed animal
while playing in nature.

2

Take a photo or
ask someone to help
you take one.

WE WILL RECOGNIZE YOUR CREATIVITY AND WILL LOVE

ANIMAL FRIENDS TOO!

Here's how in four easy steps:

3

Upload and share your
photo on our page,
Facebook.com/ellieandpudgy

4

Tell us their names
and type
hashtag #elliesfriends

MEETING YOUR FAVORITE STUFFED ANIMAL FRIENDS TOO!

Activity Solutions

page 38

page 39

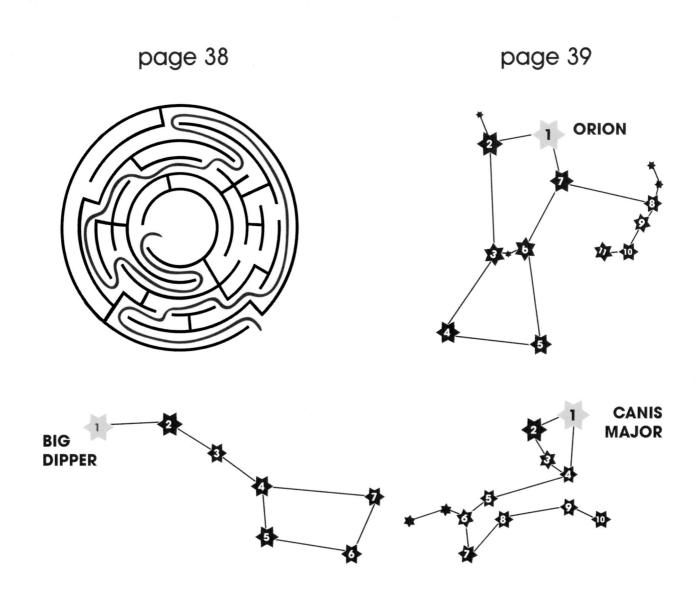

ORION

BIG
DIPPER

CANIS
MAJOR

Parents,

How can we teach our children to respect and protect nature?
Big or small, we can all help! Here are some things your children can do:

🌿 **Save water**. Turn off the faucet when you brush your teeth and take a shorter shower. (eartheasy.com)

🌿 **Plant a tree**. Trees help keep our air clean, produce oxygen for us to breathe, provide homes for animals, and much more. (treepeople.org).

🌿 **Turn off lights**. It saves electricity and even water. It can take over four gallons of water to keep a sixty watt lightbulb lit for twelve hours. (nature.org)

🌿 **Help pick up litter**. Make it fun with friends, create art from recycling, and share your cleaned up success. (doinggoodtogether.com)

🌿 **Go on a hike**. Take your friends and family. People protect what they care about! (nationalgeographic.com)

Marci and Elle | #elliesfriends

The Amazing Adventures of Ellie The Elephant
- Ellie Camps Under the Stars -

Copyright ©2016 Marci Fair, Pacochel Press LLC
All rights reserved. First edition. Printed in the United States of America.

Photographed in Highlands, North Carolina.

Permission to reproduce or transmit in any form or by any means—electronic or mechanical, including photocopying and recording—or by any information storage and retrieval system, must be obtained by contacting the author by email at info@guiltfreemom.com.

Ordering Information
For additional copies contact your favorite bookstore, online store, or email info@guiltfreemom.com.
Special offers for large orders are available.

ISBN-10: 0-9963635-3-X
ISBN-13: 978-0-9963635-3-2

Elle has grown up a lot since we started these books when she was eight! It has been an adventure that we will never forget. Who knows what adventures we will share together next!

www.EllieAdventures.com

Made in the USA
Monee, IL
11 December 2019

18435324R00026